This Walker book belongs to:

_____

_____

_____

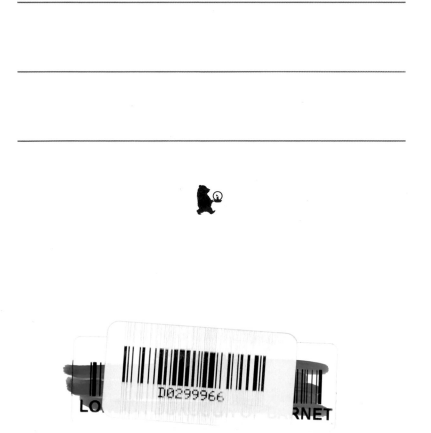

To all the little Fridas in the world

First published 2019 by Walker Books Ltd, 87 Vauxhall Walk, London SE11 5HJ

This edition published 2020

2 4 6 8 10 9 7 5 3 1

© 2019 Brun Ltd

The right of Anthony Browne to be identified as author/illustrator of this work has been
asserted by him in accordance with the Copyright, Designs and Patents Act 1988

This book has been typeset in Plantin
Printed in China

British Library Cataloguing in Publication Data: a catalogue record for
this book is available from the British Library

ISBN 978-1-4063-9091-9

www.walker.co.uk

Little Frida

ANTHONY BROWNE

WALKER BOOKS
AND SUBSIDIARIES
LONDON • BOSTON • SYDNEY • AUCKLAND

When I was six I fell ill with polio and

had to stay in bed for nine months. It was

extremely painful and when I eventually got

better I could only walk slowly, with

a limp. Other children laughed and made

fun of me, calling me "Peg-Leg!" whenever

I walked past.

I tried to hide my thin right leg with three

layers of socks, but it didn't fool anybody.

I was different and being different made

me an outsider.

My father was a photographer and

sometimes he let me help him in his studio.

I coloured up many of his black-and-white

photographs. Although it was boring work

I loved being together with him.

Most days though, in spite of having

three sisters, I played on my own. I was

lonely, but I quite liked being separate.

When I slept I dreamed of flying. I longed to really fly.

I thought about it all the time and for my seventh birthday

I asked my parents for a toy plane. For days I could think

of nothing else but flying right around the world…

But when the day finally came, these wings were all I got...

I didn't want to show my disappointment so I kept

the stupid wings on and ran to my room.

As I breathed on the window it slowly became

misty with condensation. I idly drew a shape on the

glass with my finger. Then I added a handle,

and suddenly it was a door!

I opened the door, and stepped through it. I was FREE.

I could run!

I ran and ran and ran until I was completely exhausted.

I was hot and very thirsty and there in
front of me was a dairy. I walked all round
the building looking for a way in but
I couldn't see one.

Just when I was about to give up and go home

I noticed a little door. I crawled inside.

And then

I seemed

to be falling

slowly

down into

the depths

of the earth.

At the bottom a girl was waiting for me. She didn't say anything, not even "Hello", but in a strange way I felt as if I'd known her all my life.

I smiled at her and she smiled too.

The girl silently started to dance. She was a beautiful dancer and while she gracefully danced around the room I talked to her. I told her all the secret things I worried about (there were many), and she listened to every word I said.

The girl was a stranger, but she felt so
familiar. We sat and laughed together.
I laughed very loudly and she laughed
without making a sound. We quickly
became the closest friends.

I'd never had a friend before.
It was a wonderful feeling.

After a while I knew I had to go. We waved goodbye

and I flew back home, away from the dairy …

across the plains, and through the door drawn on

the window. I rubbed out the door and ran to the

furthest corner of the garden.

I sat there and thought about my
journey and my new friend.
I was alone again, but now I was
very happy. I knew that I could
go back and see her whenever
I wanted. She would be there
waiting for me.

From that day I began to paint
the girl, over and over again.
I've visited her many times since
that day, and in a way, I've been
painting her ever since…

Frida Kahlo

Frida Kahlo was born and lived in Mexico for most of her life. Much of her work, with its distinctive style and vibrant colour, was inspired by the nature and folk art of Mexico, and by her own often painful life experiences. Her childhood was plagued by illness and injury – when Frida was six years old she contracted polio, leaving her with a limp. After being isolated for months by the illness she was then bullied by her peers. Then, as a teenager, Kahlo suffered near fatal injuries in a bus accident, which caused her severe health problems for the rest of her life. These experiences meant that Frida was acutely conscious of her otherness and the difference between her inner and outer worlds.

Around the time she had polio, when she was about six years old, Frida invented an imaginary friend who could dance without limping. In her diary she described her first meeting with this companion, from flying through a door she drew on her window and descending into the earth under a dairy, to sharing secrets with a friend who danced and laughed without making a sound.

Frida Kahlo grew up to become one of the most celebrated artists in the world. She painted many striking self-portraits that mixed reality with fantasy and credited some of her paintings to the memory of this imaginary friend. One of these is "The Two Fridas" (1939), an unusual double self-portrait created during her divorce from fellow artist Diego Rivera. In her diary Frida described the work as being inspired by the "magic friendship" that she experienced as a child.

Anthony Browne

Anthony Browne is one of the most celebrated author–illustrators of his generation. Acclaimed Children's Laureate from 2009 to 2011 and winner of multiple awards – including the prestigious Kate Greenaway Medal and the much coveted Hans Christian Andersen Award – Anthony is renowned for his unique style. His work is loved around the world.

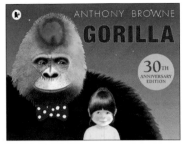

ISBN 978-1-4063-5233-7

ISBN 978-1-84428-559-4

ISBN 978-1-4063-1328-4

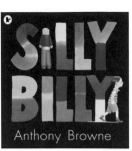

ISBN 978-1-4063-0576-0

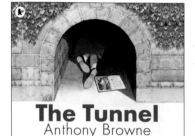

ISBN 978-1-4063-1329-1

ISBN 978-1-4063-1930-9

ISBN 978-1-4063-1852-4

ISBN 978-0-7445-9858-2

ISBN 978-1-4063-3851-5
ISBN 978-1-4063-4791-3
Board book edition

ISBN 978-0-7445-9857-5
ISBN 978-1-4063-2178-4
Board book edition

ISBN 978-1-4063-2628-4

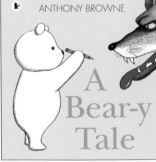

ISBN 978-1-4063-7383-7

ISBN 978-1-4063-5641-0

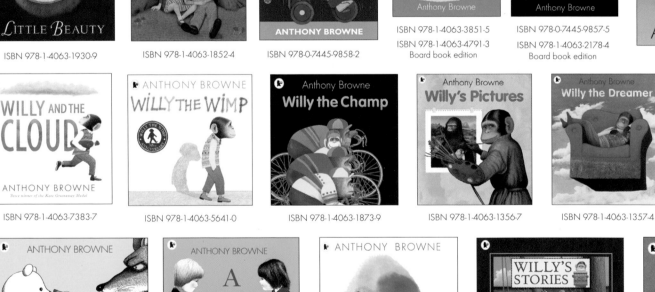

ISBN 978-1-4063-1873-9

ISBN 978-1-4063-1356-7

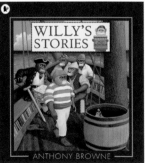

ISBN 978-1-4063-1357-4

ISBN 978-1-4063-1339-0

ISBN 978-1-4063-4162-1

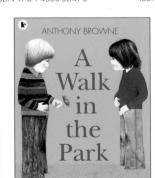

ISBN 978-1-4063-4164-5

ISBN 978-1-4063-4533-9

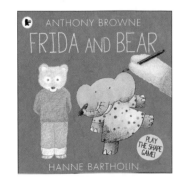

ISBN 978-1-4063-6089-9

ISBN 978-1-4063-6557-3

Available from all good booksellers

www.walker.co.uk